The Witch With The Glitch

A Lost Bookshop Adventure

by Adam Maxwell

For Nina

(the real one)

1

The Hidden Room In The Lost Bookshop

The children had come to the Lost Bookshop looking for an adventure. It wasn't every weekend that Nina, her best friend Ivy, and Oswald (who Nina used to know as 'that boy who hangs around the bookshop') were all together in the shop. But on this particular Saturday, they were.

And on this Saturday, Nina's Uncle Bill had them all working hard, tidying up different sections of the bookshop. Ivy had arrived as the shop opened, her parents dropped her off as Nina turned the sign on the door from 'closed' to 'open', and Oswald had turned up not long after. Oswald took the bus in spite of being a year younger than the girls. He always said that his parents didn't care what he did. Nina thought that might be because they were the sort of parents who were safe in the knowledge their son was the sort of boy who hung out in bookshops and libraries.

Well, that's what they *thought* anyway.

Nina and Ivy knew differently because they had been on the adventures too. Taming lions, Wild West shootouts, pirates, ninjas, fairies, lost castles, found treasure, under seas and over skies. If the grown-ups *had* known anything they would have…

Well, they probably would have made the

children tidy up the bookshop instead of going into the hidden room.

"What I don't understand," said Nina, as she poked her head through a doorway to see Ivy moving a dusty stack of books from one side of the room to the other, one or two at a time, "is how he can tell if we've tidied up at all."

Ivy smiled and pushed her blond hair out of her eyes as she looked up at her best friend. "I don't know," she replied. "But somehow he knows."

"He has no idea about this, though." Nina waved a silver key at Ivy. It hung from a chain around her neck.

Ivy knew it was the key to the hidden room. The room that had remained undiscovered until Uncle Bill had found it behind an ancient bookshelf. The room that only the children had ever entered. The room that led to untold adventures.

"I've still got to sort all these books out," said Ivy, pointing towards the stacks and stacks of unsorted hardbacks and paperbacks all piled precariously on the floor. "How did you finish so quickly anyway?"

"Oh it was easy," said Nina with a wicked grin.

"Tell me!"

"How many rooms are in the bookshop?" asked Nina.

"Oh, I don't know," said Ivy, standing up and dusting herself down. "It's impossible to say. Sometimes I think I know, and then I turn down a corridor and it's like I've never been there before. It's as if they move."

Nina laughed. "Exactly," she said. "So the chances of Uncle Bill remembering which room he asked you to tidy are this big…" Nina held up her index finger and thumb and showed Ivy a gap so small they almost touched.

Ivy nodded.

"And," Nina continued, "when you've finished tidying how do the rooms look?"

"Pretty much the same," said Ivy with a smile.

Nina nodded.

"But just in case, give me a hand and we'll do one little thing…" Nina trailed off as she got down on her hands and knees next to the stacks of books Ivy still had to sort out. "Well…come on!"

Ivy realised what her friend was up to and hopped down next to her. The pair of them carefully pushed the stacks of books across the floor from one side of the room to the other.

Nina hopped to her feet. "There!" she exclaimed. "All done. And no-one will be any the wiser."

"No-one will be any the wiser about what?" said a voice.

Both of the girls jumped in fright and spun around to face the door. They breathed a sigh of relief when they saw it was Oswald.

"Oswald!" said Ivy.

"Don't sneak around like that," said Nina. "You gave me a fright!"

"Did you cheat as well?" asked Ivy sheepishly.

"Cheat at what?" asked Oswald. Then, noticing what the girls were doing, he added, "Certainly not! I did it quickly. I know where all the—"

"Okay, okay we get the idea," Nina interrupted. "Anyway, let's go!"

Nina shoved past Oswald and out into the corridor, picking up speed as she did so. Ivy followed suit and Oswald twisted around, nearly losing his small, round glasses. He pushed them back up onto his face before jogging after the girls.

It was surprising how quickly they could move, considering all the obstacles that surrounded them. You see, the bookshop wasn't simply filled with books. Oh no. It was bursting with them. The shelves that had originally lined the walls of each of the rooms and side rooms had spread to the corridors, and eventually to every upright surface in the shop.

And then more bookshelves had grown from the floors in the middle of room until they too had filled with small books, large books, paperback books, hardback books, books with pictures, books with only words, long books, short books. Books, books and more books!

Once the shelves had been filled, they piled the books by the sides and on the floors until it was difficult to step anywhere without your foot or your leg nudging the edge of a story. But because it was Nina's Aunty Ann and Uncle Bill who owned the Lost Bookshop, Nina had been there on and off for her whole life. The gaps between the books were practically her footsteps and so she stepped fast and sure, moving purposefully forward with Ivy and Oswald struggling a little to keep up.

Soon they skidded around a corner and reached an old wooden door with a sign that said 'staff only'. Nina flung it open and ran through, stopping suddenly at the top of a wooden spiral staircase. Her eyes flashed as she hopped up onto the bannister and slid, round and round, down and down, all the way to the bottom.

"Come on!" she cried, waiting for her friends to follow.

Ivy hopped on and sped down the bannister, giggling as she spiralled down, round and round, hopping off at the bottom more than a little dizzy. Oswald shook his head and ran down the steps, taking them two at a time.

"Scaredy cat!" said Nina, sticking her tongue out at him.

Oswald crossed his eyes and stuck his tongue out right back at her.

The three children laughed as they pushed open the downstairs door and found themselves in Uncle Bill's office, an open fire roaring in the hearth opposite the door.

"I didn't realise this door came out here," said Oswald, scratching his head.

Nina shrugged. "Apparently it does today."

There was a cough from the other side of the room. It was Uncle Bill, sat behind a large wooden desk piled high with books.

"Mischief?" was the only word he said.

Nina didn't answer. Instead she shook her head before running over to him and planting a great big kiss right on his cheek.

"Your beard tickles," she giggled. "And we've finished tidying, so can we play now?"

"There's no way you lot—" he began.

"Billy, if they've finished let them have some fun!" Aunty Ann's voice floated in from somewhere nearby. "What mischief could they possibly get up to in the bookshop? And anyway, the kettle's just boiled."

Uncle Bill nodded, stood up and scratched absently at his grey beard. "A nice cup of tea wouldn't go amiss about now," he said.

The children looked at one another excitedly, but when they turned back Uncle

Bill had vanished.

"How does he do that?" asked Oswald.

Nina shrugged, then sneaked stealthily out of the room with the other two children creeping after her.

A twist and a turn later and Nina, Ivy and Oswald were standing in front of the door to the hidden room. Nina whipped the key out, jammed it in the lock and turned it. A familiar rusty, clanking noise shuddered through the air as the old mechanism unlocked the door.

There was a loud creak that the children could feel in the pits of their tummies as Nina pushed it slowly open, followed by a strange hiss that sounded a little like a snake sighing. The children could smell dust, and something else. Something that was different. Chocolate? Or sweeties perhaps?

Whatever it was, they didn't have time to stop and think about it – the grown-ups might find them at any second. The three friends piled into the hidden room and slammed the door, shutting it tight.

Usually there was light in the hidden room, trickling down through the dust from windows high above the shelves. But today, as the door clunked closed, the children couldn't see their own hands in front of their faces. Oswald took a tentative step forward but tripped over Ivy's foot. He tumbled forward, putting out his hands to break his fall, and as he did so his fingers caught a book, falling too.

"Uh oh," he said, holding the book in front of his face and trying to make out what it was

"What?" one of the girls asked, but it was too late. Dust swirled around the room, picking up speed, spinning and spinning. The room lurched and the children staggered, stumbling forward as the world spun round and round until, with a thunderous bang, the spinning stopped and everything went dark.

2

Magic In The Woods

The children walked forwards in the darkness for a few steps and almost at once became aware that the ground under their feet, which should have been solid wooden floorboards, now felt more spongy and springy.

A few more cautious steps and the light had returned, ever-so slightly. Beneath their shoes they could see what looked like grass and patches of brown earth.

Nina pushed forward, moving something out of the way, and, just like that, sunlight came streaming down. She looked at what she had moved and found a bunch of overhanging branches and leaves. Turning around, she could see the others behind her. They were coming out of deep, dark woods and into a clearing in a forest.

"A forest," Ivy nodded. "That's new."

"What did you expect?" Nina's eyes flashed with mischief. "A room full of books?"

Oswald ducked a low-hanging branch, but a twig caught his glasses, whipping them off and boinging them forward past Nina and into the clearing.

"Oh great," he grumbled. "Can anyone see where they went? I can't find them without them."

Ivy darted forward, her blonde ponytail

narrowly missing getting caught too. She spotted the glasses lying next to a cluster of bright red toadstools.

"Here they are!" she said, picking them up and giving them a wipe on her t-shirt just like she'd seen Oswald do so many times before. But her mouth fell open in surprise and she pointed at something on the edge of the clearing. "Oh my goodness. Look at that!"

"What? What?" cried Oswald. "I can't see."

He grabbed his glasses, popped them back on, and immediately everything came back into focus. But it wasn't exactly what he had expected. On the edge of the clearing was a house. It had a brown door, as you might expect, but the walls were bright pink with white spots all over and the roof…well, the roof was like a multi-coloured mixed-up rainbow of bobbles and swirls. Oswald blinked and gave his glasses another rub just to be sure, but it didn't make much difference. No matter how hard he stared, he was one hundred per cent sure that the house was made of sweets.

As the children edged closer and closer they could see it in better and better detail. The door was made of chocolate, the walls covered with cake icing and spotted with white chocolate buttons. Candy rock and candy canes framed the windows and in every available gap there were lollipops and sugar dusted jellies and...

"Wow," said Nina. "That's a lot of sweets."

"I don't think I've ever seen that many sweets in my whole, entire life," added Ivy.

"What do you think happens when it rains?" asked Oswald, who was a practical-minded sort of boy. "Do you think it all melts?"

"I expect it's magic," said Nina. "You can't just build a house out of sweets. Something like this has to be magic."

Ivy nodded. "And I expect they've thought of the whole rain issue."

"So if it's magic I expect we shouldn't eat it then?" asked Oswald as he edged closer to the house. "Not even a little bit?"

He reached out his hand, but Ivy gave it a little smack.

"No!" she snapped. "You've read fairytales before. If we eat the house—"

But Ivy didn't get the chance to finish because suddenly the candy house made a noise that sounded like *whurp ping!* The children turned to see what was going on and, as they did, a pink mist flew out of a window and zapped straight into them.

Nina, Ivy and Oswald were knocked to the ground like pins in a bowling alley.

"Ow!" said Oswald, rubbing his chest where the magical force had hit him.

"What was that?" asked Ivy.

"Urrrgh," grumbled Nina. "Magic, I guess. And we didn't even do anything."

The children got to their feet and Oswald and Nina dusted themselves down. But Ivy didn't. She swayed slightly and rubbed her head. Something wasn't right. Something was different. And not in a good way.

Ivy was about to tell the others how funny she felt, but when she looked over she saw Nina leaning towards Oswald's neck. It was as if she was in a trance – her mouth was wide open and, if Ivy wasn't mistaken, Nina had developed two long, pointy fangs.

"Hey!" she shouted. "What are you doing?"

Nina looked up, distracted and confused. Ivy ran towards them, but Oswald had obviously got a fright when she shouted. He jumped out of the way, then something even more peculiar happened.

Oswald's nose began to grow, his chin too, in fact his whole body seemed to shift and, as it did, a thick grey fur developed. His clothes began to stretch, almost bursting at the seams as he dropped down on to all fours, no longer looking much like the friend they knew. Now he looked more like a wolf. A werewolf.

"No, no, no!" said Ivy and, staggering forward, she tripped over her own feet. She tumbled head over heels but, instead of bumping into Nina and Oswald, she passed straight through them. As she fell further forward she closed her eyes, expecting to hit the hard candy of the walls, but instead she passed straight through them too.

Ivy came to rest in the parlour of the gingerbread house. She stood still for a moment, trying to work out what had happened.

"Oh great," said a voice she didn't recognise. "A ghost. That's all I need. Go on, get knotted, you can't come in here to haunt my house! Go on, shoo!"

3

Ghostly Goings-On

Ivy reached up and touched her brow. It felt normal. A little cold perhaps, but a moment ago they had been outside in the woods. She seemed quite solid.

Which was more than a little worrying since all the evidence was pointing to the fact that she could no longer touch anything. For instance, at that very moment she wasn't just standing in the parlour of the candy house. No. She was standing in the middle of a table in the parlour of the candy house.

Her legs and her feet were underneath the

table. The tabletop passed straight through her tummy and the top of her was above the table. Ivy moved her hand towards one of the chairs, hoping to push it out of the way, but her hand passed right through as if it wasn't there at all.

"Are you quite finished?" the voice piped up again. "I'm actually in the middle of something important here."

Finally, Ivy turned around and, by the fire on the other side of the parlour, was a woman in a rocking chair. She was almost normal looking, young-ish and pretty, but there were three slightly odd things about her.

Firstly, her skin was bright green like the colour of leaves on a tree. Secondly, she wore a black, pointed hat and, thirdly, in her hand was a long, wooden stick. A wand, Ivy thought.

"You did this!" Ivy snapped, suddenly getting very cross at the woman, who might have been a witch.

"What?" the witchy woman shouted. "No! Why would you say that?"

Ivy stormed over to the green-skinned lady and pointed a finger towards her.

"Why would I say that?" Ivy shouted. "Why? Well, that's quite simple. Because a moment ago me and my two friends were outside admiring your candy house and *whoosh* – some magical force wallops us and... and... something has happened to all of us."

Ivy stood waving her finger at the witch. She was so cross her face had turned bright red.

"Ah," said the witch quietly. "That might have been a little bit to do with me."

"A little bit?" Ivy snapped. "You turned me into a ghost!"

"Ah."

"I'm not even dead!"

"Oh."

"And I think my best friend might be a vampire."

"Erm."

"And my other friend is probably a werewolf."

"Oops." The witch lifted the front of her pointy hat and scratched her head. "Yes, that sounds a bit like something that was possibly completely my fault."

"Possibly completely your fault?" asked

Ivy in confusion. "What does that even mean?"

"Weeeeeeeeell..." said the green-skinned lady, then she sighed an enormous sigh and sank deeper into her chair.

"Let me take a wild guess here," said Ivy. She was about to stamp her foot but was afraid it might go through the floor. "You're a witch?"

The witch nodded.

"And this..." Ivy waved at herself. "This is an accident?"

The witch nodded again.

"Well," said Ivy. "I'll pop out and get my friends then you can turn us back to normal."

Before the witch could say anything, Ivy walked silently through the table, through the chair and finally through the wall to the outside. It was more than a little strange moving around without being able to hear even the slightest tip tap of your own footsteps, but Ivy was so angry that she was prepared to accept it, at least for a few minutes.

She walked up to Nina and tried to tap her on the shoulder. Except her hand went straight through her best friend's shoulder and Nina didn't even realise.

"Poo sandwiches!" Ivy shouted in frustration.

Nina screamed in fright, and Ivy wasn't sure but she could have sworn that she heard a dog whimper somewhere nearby.

"Who the—" Nina said, spinning around to face Ivy. "It's you!"

Nina gave her friend a big smile and Ivy noticed that the sharp vampire teeth had disappeared. At least for now.

"Where's Oswald?" asked Ivy.

"Why did you shout 'poo sandwiches' at me?" asked Nina.

"No time for that," said Ivy impatiently. "There's a witch in that house. She did this to us and she's going to turn us back."

There was a scampering sound nearby, and out of the undergrowth bounded a wolf with small, round glasses, holding a stick in its mouth. Ivy cried out in shock as the wolf jumped up at her, but she needn't have worried. Just as Ivy had passed through the wall, the wolf passed through Ivy. But the wolf wasn't a ghost and so it hit the wall with a crunch and slid down to the ground, where it transformed back into someone a little more familiar.

"Oswald?" said Ivy in surprise.

Oswald jumped to his feet, the stick still held between his teeth, his clothes a little ragged but somehow shrinking back to his normal size.

"What were you doing?" Ivy asked her two friends.

"Erm," said Nina sheepishly. "Playing fetch."

"Playing fetch?" Ivy's voice was getting higher and higher. "This is no time to play fetch! Come with me!"

Ivy stomped off up the gingerbread house's path and straight through the chocolate door.

"You'll have to let yourselves in," she

shouted from inside.

Nina opened the door and Oswald walked in, still holding the stick awkwardly in his hand. The witch stood up from her chair and walked towards the children. Nina tried to walk through the doorway but something stopped her.

She took a step backwards and tried again but, once again, it was as if there was a glass wall in her way. She pressed her face against the invisible barrier, smooshing her lips into it and sticking her tongue out.

Oswald giggled.

"Mwhy cnt I cm in?" said Nina.

"What have you done now?" Ivy asked the witch in a very bossy tone of voice.

"I haven't done anything!" said the witch. "Oh, hang on..."

The witch pointed at each of them in turn.

"Ghost. Werewolf. Vampire," she said. "That'll be it. Your friend out there is the vampire?"

Ivy nodded.

"Vampires can't come in to houses unless you invite them," said the witch with a knowing nod.

"Come on in," said Ivy.

Nina walked forward but whacked into the invisible barrier once more.

"Ow!" she said.

"You have to be the one who owns the house to invite a vampire in," the witch continued.

"Well, if you're going to magic us all back to normal you had better invite her in," said

Ivy firmly.

The witch nodded. Then she shook her head.

"Back to normal?" she asked eventually. "No, I'm afraid I can't turn you back to normal. You're stuck like this."

4

What Does A Gingerbread House Taste Like?

"Noooooooo!" Oswald howled, the words starting out human but sounding more like a dog the longer he shouted.

Ivy glared at him. He gave a little whimper and, even though at that moment he was back to being a boy, scampered over to stand in the corner.

"Oh, don't stand out there looking like a tomato squashed against a window," the witch chuckled as she pointed to Nina. "If your friends are in you might as well come in too. I invite you."

Nina pushed her hand forward. The invisible barrier was no longer there, so she edged her way inside and shut the door behind her.

"Thank you," she said. "Now what do you mean by saying we're stuck this way?"

"Just that, I'm afraid, my lovelies." The witch gave a smile and a sigh and wandered back to her chair by the fire. "It would seem I'm not a very good witch anymore."

Nina glanced over at Ivy, who was floating half in and half out of a dining chair. She could see that her friend was getting mad. If she was honest she was pretty mad herself, but shouting wouldn't do them any good. She took a deep breath and walked over by the fire next to the witch.

"I'm Nina," said Nina. "This is Ivy and Oswald."

The witch nodded. "I'm Belinda," she said.

"I don't mean to be rude," said Nina. "But did you cast the spell that turned us all this way?"

The witch nodded.

"And you can't turn us back?"

The witch shook her head.

"But why ever not?" Ivy snapped.

The witch stared at the three of them, a confused look passing over her face like a cloud raining frowns.

"You've got no idea who I am, do you?" she asked eventually.

"Nope," said Oswald.

"Nuh-uh," said Ivy.

"Sorry, we're not from around here," said Nina.

"Have you tasted the house?" Belinda the witch asked.

The children shook their heads.

The witch told them to have a try, so both Nina and Oswald snapped off a couple of delicious-looking treats that decorated the mantelpiece. Ivy simply stood in the middle of the chair she was haunting and glared at them. At least until Nina and Oswald bit into the sweeties.

"Bleurgh!" the pair shouted.

Ivy giggled as she watched her two friends trying to scrape the vile taste from their tongues.

"Eew," said Nina. "That is absolutely disgusting."

The witch nodded.

"It wasn't even supposed to be a candy house," she added. "All I wanted was a lemon meringue pie. I waved my wand, said my spell and whoosh... a candy covered house which gets sticky when it rains and tastes like a pile of dog's poo."

Ivy laughed again. Nina looked like she might be sick.

"So how did this happen?" Ivy managed, after taking a breath to push her giggles down inside herself. "And how did you manage to turn us into...into...monsters?"

"All I thought was I might try a little spell for Halloween, you know, decorate the place with some spooky dolls?" she replied. "And I waved my wand, said my spell and..."

"And?"

"And the people in the village call me the witch with the glitch."

"Seems like a fair description," Oswald whispered to Ivy.

The witch glared at him and flicked her wand in his direction. Red sparks danced from the end and Oswald went back to whimpering in the corner.

"All I wanted to do was to make the place all spooky," Belinda the witch said. "I thought if I did, the villagers might stop believing I was going to do something horrid to them and maybe let me join in the trick or treating and the Halloween spirit."

"Spirit. Hahaha," Oswald chuckled, prodding his finger through the middle of Ivy's ghostly head.

"Oi!" said Ivy, moving her head out of

the way.

"Eew," said Oswald, looking at the strange ectoplasm-goo that was now on his finger.

"Everything's gone wrong," Belinda continued. "Ever since I got here it's been one thing after another. First the house, then Izzy, then... then..." The witch held up her bright green hand and stared intently at it for a second. "All I wanted was a nice bubble bath." She let out a long, sad, sigh.

"You mean..." said Nina cautiously. "That you...I mean to say...your skin isn't supposed to be...green?"

The witch closed her eyes and leaned toward Oswald. "Has your friend had a bump on the head recently?" she asked.

"Ummmm," said Oswald.

The witch opened her eyes. "WHAT A STUPID QUESTION!" she screamed at the top of her lungs. "OF COURSE MY SKIN ISN'T SUPPOSED TO BE GREEN!!"

"Sorry," Nina whispered.

The witch took a deep breath and stared at the three of them.

"Excuse me, Miss Belinda," Ivy decided that being polite might be the best course of action after all. "Is there anything we can do to stop you… erm… glitching?"

The witch picked up her wand once more, turning it over absent-mindedly in her hands.

Ivy thought for a moment about disappearing through the nearest wall, but the witch finally looked up at her. As she did, the corners of her mouth turned up ever-so slightly into the beginnings of a smile.

"Izzy," she said.

"Izzy?" Ivy asked.

"If you find Izzy and bring her to me…" the witch trailed off.

"Then you'll turn yourself… erm… not green?" asked Nina.

Belinda nodded.

"And you'll turn the house not poo-flavoured?" asked Oswald.

Belinda nodded.

"And you'll turn us back to children again?" ask Ivy.

The witch sighed, then she nodded. "There's one more thing. The spell will need to be reversed before midnight. If it isn't, then there really will be nothing we can do and you'll be stuck that way forever. Now, be off with you, get out of my house before I change my mind," she said.

So they did.

5

Follow The
Pebble People-Path

Nina and Oswald walked out of the front door of the witch's house. Ivy tried her best to do the same, but the wind caught the door, slamming it shut and passing right though her like a knife through butter. She looked down at her body. She could still see it and feel it but the world around her felt more like clouds. She *saw* everything perfectly but she couldn't *touch* it. Every time she reached out to try, her hand passed straight through.

"I don't like this," said Ivy, floating closer to Nina. "It's scary."

Nina stopped and looked at her friend. Ivy was there alright, but if Nina looked closely she could see the witch's gingerbread house through her friend.

"I would give you a hug..." Nina trailed off, but seeing that her best friend might burst into tears she knew she had to try something different. "Hey, watch this!"

Nina crept over to Oswald, who was on his hands and knees sniffing at a nearby tree. She tiptoed closer and closer and then...

"Boo!" she shouted.

Oswald didn't get a fright. He didn't even turn around. Instead, he kept sniffing at the tree.

"You can't scare me," he said, touching

the bark of the tree. "I think I must have special werewolf powers because…"

Oswald turned around and screamed like a little baby girl.

Ivy burst out laughing. "How did you scare him?" she asked.

Nina turned around to reveal two long fang-like teeth which had grown, seemingly from nowhere, in her mouth.

"Oh, don't be a baby, Oswald," she said. She ran her tongue over her new gnashers and gave a big, white grin. "I wouldn't bite you."

Oswald stared at Nina suspiciously. "You wouldn't?" he asked, unconvinced.

"Hmmm. Probably not. Unless I was really hungry!" Nina lunged forward, pretending to grab him. Oswald ducked but lost his footing and fell into the trees that surrounded the clearing.

Nina and Ivy burst into a fit of giggles.

"Nina," said Ivy between laughs. "How are we going to find this 'Izzy' person the witch was talking about?"

"That's the least of our worries," said Nina, managing to stop laughing but still showing off a huge too-toothy grin. "We're going to need to find that Oswald person before we do anything else. Unless he's turned back into a doggy and he's having a wee against a tree."

"Hey!" said Oswald, poking his human-face through the undergrowth. "I'm not... doing my business in the woods."

"Do werewolves wee in the woods?" asked Ivy with another giggle.

"I've found a path," said Oswald, suddenly sounding very serious.

Nina gave her head a slow left-right shake and her vampire fangs vanished. "Now I remember why we keep you around, Oswald," she said. "You're very useful a lot of the time. Where's this path then?"

Oswald's head vanished back into the bushes, then there was a rustling sound before he popped out again a few metres further away.

"Here," he said. "Look!"

The girls ran and floated over to where Oswald's head was visible. Nina pushed through the bushes and held them back for Ivy to try to make her feel like a real person again. Ivy thanked her as she passed from the light of the clearing into the gloom of the woods.

It took the girls a moment for their eyes to become accustomed to the half-light. Once their sight had adjusted they could see Oswald standing next to a single, white, stone around the size of a gobstopper.

"Don't say it," said Oswald, his eyebrows crunching together into a frown.

"It's just…" said Ivy.

"Don't say it."

"Well… erm…" Nina smirked.

"Don't say it," Oswald said again. "I know what you're going to—"

"That's not a path, it's a pebble!" blurted Nina.

Oswald shook his head and wandered away from the girls. "I told you not to say it," he muttered to himself. "But you couldn't resist, could you?"

"It's not so much a people-path as a pixie-path," said Ivy, floating up to join Oswald. "Oh... hang on a minute..."

Ivy pointed and as Nina caught up with her she saw a trail of white pebbles. She was about to make another joke when she saw that a few metres away the path doubled in width, then doubled again and again and again until, at the point it faded into the darkness of the forest, it was wide enough for the children to walk side by side.

"Sorry Oswald," said Nina.

"I told you not to say anything," he replied.

"Sorry Oswald," said Ivy.

"Right then," said Nina, clapping her hands. "Are we going to see where it leads?"

And with that she ran as fast as she possibly could, following the bright white path onward to wherever it led.

"Oi!" Ivy and Oswald chorused, then they both burst into action, sprinting after their friend.

It didn't take long for Oswald to catch up. His new werewolf legs, although not wolfed-out, felt different. Stronger, perhaps. He powered forward, catching up with Ivy and racing past towards Nina.

They laughed and joked and shouted as they ran, sending woodland creatures fluttering and scampering in fright as they bounded onward. Soon, the path started to get narrower and narrower. The three of them stopped when they noticed it was shrinking down to a single stone wide once more.

"Do you think that's the edge of the woods?" asked Ivy nervously.

Oswald nodded. "Reckon so, yeah," he replied.

The three children stood, Nina and Oswald panting lightly and Ivy hovering, accidentally a few centimetres above the ground.

"What do you think we'll find out there?" Oswald went on.

"Not sure," said Nina, taking a deep breath. "Only one way to find out, though."

Nina darted forward beyond the end of the path and popped her head out of the woods. A couple of seconds ticked by and then she dipped back into the woods.

"What did you see?" asked Ivy.

"People," said Nina.

"Oh good," said Oswald.

Nina shook her head, then poked it out of the woods once more. This time there was a roaring noise from the other side.

"Not good," said Nina, turning back to Ivy and Oswald. "Very, very, very not good."

She was about to say something else when an enormous hand reached through the undergrowth and, grabbing her by the scruff of the neck, dragged her out of sight and off who-knew-where?

6

Nina Goes Batty

Ivy screamed. Oswald threw his hand up to cover her mouth, but his hand passed straight through her ghostly head, leaving him to topple forward onto the soil and grass of the forest floor. She stared at him goggle-eyed as he wiped the ghost-gloop from his hand onto a small patch of moss next to where he'd fallen.

"Shhh," he whispered.

Ivy mouthed the word, "Sorry."

Oswald beckoned Ivy over and she floated to his side.

"Did you see what grabbed Nina?" he whispered.

Ivy shook her head.

"After three we run out to save her?"

Ivy looked over to the spot where Nina had vanished. When she looked back Oswald was no longer Oswald; he was a big, grey, snarling, werewolf. With a small, round pair of glasses perched on the end of his nose and some increasingly raggedy clothes barely covering his wolfy body. She would have reached out and taken them, put them in her pocket, but she was getting the hang of the fact that it wouldn't work.

"One…" Ivy began.

Oswald-wolf nodded his wolfy-nose.

"Two…" Ivy continued slowly.

"*Woof!*" Oswald barked, and then

bounded towards the edge of the woods.

I guess that means three, Ivy thought before zipping after him.

When she passed through the trees and out of the forest Ivy was greeted by a very odd sight indeed. She saw the outskirts of a village; as the forest ended, the streets, houses and shops began. The children could see signs hanging outside; a bakery, a blacksmith and even a little bookshop. But that wasn't the odd part. An enormous crowd of people, perhaps a hundred or more, were all gathered, waiting, at the edge where the village met the forest. There were men, women and children, tall and short, thin and fat, and they all had the strangest things in their hands.

Some people carried feather dusters,

others carried cushions or pillows. Over there was a woman with a pair of slippers, one in each hand. Towards the back of the crowd Ivy could see a tall man with big, wet, fish, which he waved menacingly above his head. There was a woman who looked quite like Oswald's mum, carrying a pair of bellows. She gave them the occasional squeeze as she stared at the children. Ivy squinted at these crazy people and the more she looked, the more she saw; big, fancy hats, wooden spoons. One old woman even appeared to have a live chicken in her hand and it wasn't very happy being hung upside down by its feet.

"Weird aren't they?" said a voice.

Ivy jumped in shock and spun around to see Nina standing next to her.

"Nina!" shouted Ivy. "You're alright!"

Nina nodded. "That bloke carrying the tiny, pink umbrella grabbed me but I escaped."

"*Grr-woof*," growled Oswald.

Nina looked at Oswald with his glasses perched on the end of his werewolf nose and giggled.

"Well, it turns out I can do this," she said, and with a sound like the patter of rain on leaves Nina transformed into a tiny little bat.

Oswald nodded, impressed, and his glasses began to fall off. He reached up a paw and pushed them up his wolf-snout. Ivy stared, trying to focus her eyes on the Nina-bat. Nina flapped a little closer to her face and Ivy smiled as she saw that, in spite of the wings and the fact that she was in all other ways bat-like, her best friend's face could still be seen on the creature fluttering in front of her.

"Good, eh?" said Nina, her voice tiny and really high-pitched.

Ivy nodded, impressed.

The pitter-pattering noise happened again and Nina turned back into her human-self. The crowd of onlookers all shuffled away from the children.

"I think we're frightening them," said Ivy.

Oswald nodded and his glasses fell off the end of his wolf-nose. Nina reached down and picked them up before popping them in her pocket.

"Right, here goes," said Nina, turning to face the crowd. "Hello all of you!"

The crowd grumbled a response. It was

low and unfriendly.

"You don't know us," continued Nina. "And we don't know you, but in spite of what you might think, we are very nice and we mean you no harm."

"We mean you harm," screeched the woman who was holding the chicken. The chicken squawked.

"Yeah!" a short, fat man who was holding a crumpled up bit of paper in each hand shouted in agreement. "You can't come to our village you... you... monsters!"

The word 'monsters' echoed around the crowd, repeated by people here and there.

"They've got a point," whispered Ivy. "We are *actual* monsters."

"True," said Nina quietly. "But look at them, they're a bunch of loonies. What are they even carrying?"

"*Ra-ruff,*" barked Oswald, leaning into the girls huddle so the three of them stood in a mini-circle.

"I wondered that," said Ivy. "I think they might be a mob."

"*Rawf?*" asked Oswald.

"You know," said Nina. "Like in stories – except usually they'd have flaming torches, pointy sticks, pitchforks, that sort of thing."

"So this lot aren't loonies?" asked Ivy. "They're just a really rubbish mob."

"We can hear you," said the old woman holding the chicken.

"Ah," said Nina. "Erm… sorry." She turned back to the crowd and raised her voice. "Sorry. Didn't mean to call you rubbish."

"Yes you did, I heard you!" a little boy carrying a cushion with an embroidered flower shouted back.

"Shh," Ivy hissed. "What if they try to attack us?"

Nina shrugged. "If they try to attack us with what? A chicken, a pair of slippers and a comfy cushion?" She grinned, showing her fangs once more.

Ivy stifled a laugh and looked over at the crowd. They didn't look as fierce. In fact, the longer Ivy the ghost, Nina the vampire and Oswald the werewolf stared at the mob, the more they shuffled and stirred. And the more they shuffled and stirred, the less scary they seemed to be.

"I'm not sure we should let them be scared of us," said Ivy under her breath.

"And I'm not sure wolf-boy and bat-girl are helping."

Nina looked at Ivy. Then she looked at Oswald. They both looked a little nervous in spite of the fact that they were 'monsters' too.

"You with the fire puffers," Nina said in a loud voice as she turned to the crowd. "Come over here, will you?"

"Who, me?" the woman who looked a bit like Oswald's mum asked.

Nina nodded. "Don't worry," she said. "There's no need to worry."

Several of the bigger men behind the woman shoved her towards the children.

"Watch," said Nina. She pointed to her vampire teeth.

The woman half-closed her eyes, afraid

that Nina was about to bite a chunk from her neck. Instead, Nina let the vampire teeth turn back into her normal teeth.

"See," she added. "Nothing to be afraid of. Oswald?"

Oswald gave a yap of agreement. The woman jumped in fright, then stood wide-eyed and mouth hanging open as the thick hair that covered Oswald's body disappeared, the dog-ears and wolf-nose receding back into the familiar boy-shape. Nina handed him back his glasses and he put them back on and pushed them up his nose in the way he always did. He stood up straight and stretched, smoothing down his clothes that had begun to rip and tear at the seams.

The woman stared at the two of them for

a moment before nodding her head in approval.

"What about her?" she asked, giving her bellows a puff in Ivy's direction.

"Nothing we can do about her I'm afraid," said Nina. "That's the problem."

The woman raised an eyebrow, interested but still wary of the friends.

"We're not monsters," Oswald said. "Well, we are. But not usually. This only happened recently. Less than an hour ago."

"Yes, it's true," added Ivy. "The witch zapped us and all we want is to get turned back to normal again."

The woman nodded. "Less than an hour ago?" she asked.

Nina, Ivy and Oswald all nodded.

"It isn't them," the woman shouted.

"They're not the kidnappers."

There were groans from the crowd. Some people towards the back wandered off. The woman lowered her bellows and they hissed as she squeezed the air out of them.

"What do you mean, kidnappers?" asked Ivy.

"Just that," said the woman. "Someone stole two children."

7

Help Is At Hand

Now, dear reader, I don't wish to panic you with this tale of children being transformed into mystical creatures and others being stolen from under the very noses of their parents. These things happen. Not often, of course, but they do happen and as a result you must be vigilant.

If I had a gold coin for every child who'd been magically transformed into a vampire I would be a very rich storyteller indeed. But they usually get turned back.

Well, they sometimes get turned back.

Oh, alright. A friend of mine heard a rumour that at least one of them didn't spend the rest of their life trapped in a storybook terrorising villagers and flying like bats through the night. So don't worry about it.

Stolen children, however, can fetch a pretty penny if you find the right buyer. Wolves can be relied upon to pay handsomely for freshly snatched kids (although it should be noted they prefer five year old girls). Trolls, too, are regular customers and have been known to gorge themselves on two or three children a month (again, trolls have their own preferences, apparently naughty children are the tastiest).

Two girls and one boy that were not

behaving badly were Nina, Ivy and Oswald.
In fact, Nina had explained to the crowd of
gathered villagers that, if they wanted to be a
proper lynch mob, they would need big
pitchforks and flaming torches at the very
least. Some of the mob had grumbled in
complaint but even they had hidden their
feather dusters and comfy cushions behind
their backs when they realised how wrong
they had got it.

Up close, the woman with the bellows
didn't look as much like Oswald's mum as
they had thought. Her name was Sheila and
she had explained to the friends that two
children, a boy and a girl, had gone missing
three nights ago. Search parties ventured
deep into the woods but neither of the two
children were anywhere to be found.

"Their names are Han and Greta," said Sheila. "And I'm their Aunty." She fell silent as she stared off into the darkness of the woods.

Nina, who had been listening intently to the woman, was thinking about how her family would feel if she had been missing for three days. Even the thought of it made her want to grab Sheila and give her a big hug, but she thought she'd better not in case the woman thought she was going to bite her.

"Can we help find Han and Greta?" Nina asked instead.

"What?" asked Sheila.

"What?" chorused Ivy and Oswald.

"Nina, are you sure?" asked Ivy. "I mean, I want to help as much as you but the witch said that if we don't find Izzy and get the spell reversed by midnight we would be stuck like this forever."

Oswald nodded in agreement. "She's right," he said.

"Don't worry," Nina said with a smile. "I've got an idea."

As Nina took Ivy and Oswald to one side to tell them her cunning plan, Sheila took her bellows over to the other villagers to discuss plans of their own. After a few minutes of intense discussion Sheila came back over to the children.

"What's your plan?" asked Sheila, getting straight to the point.

"Promise not to be scared?" asked Nina.

Sheila took a deep breath then nodded.

Nina stepped back and Oswald edged forward. He took off his glasses and gave them to his friend before, with a little concentration, he transformed into a werewolf once more. Sheila and the other villagers were all nervous, but they stood their ground, staring and frowning as the thick hair covered Oswald's body and his body changed into the wolf-shape.

"Oswald's a werewolf, right?" asked Nina.

Oswald made a *woof* noise in response.

"Not you, Oswald," said Nina, shaking her head. "Sorry, Sheila. Anyway a wolf's only a big dog, isn't it?"

Sheila stared at Oswald, who obediently sat down on his back legs and held out his front paw to shake. Sheila stepped forward and shook him by the paw, a look of panic on her face. Oswald nuzzled the back of her hand with his cold, wet nose.

"He's trying to say that when he's a werewolf he has a tremendous sense of smell," said Ivy with a smile. She was enjoying Oswald being a dog a lot more than she was enjoying being a ghost.

"We were thinking, if you had something that belonged to the missing children..." said Nina. "Something... that smelled of them... he could follow the scent and find them."

Sheila said nothing for a moment, then two big tears welled in her eyes.

"Come here," she said, darting forward, her arms thrown wide. She hugged the children.

Except Ivy, of course. Her arm slipped through Ivy and wound up coated in the ghostly ectoplasm.

"That's so kind of you, strangers," Sheila said eventually. "You didn't have to help, there's no reason you should. Even if you weren't going to eat us you could have easily run off. But you didn't and because of that we'll help you."

"You will?" asked Ivy.

"*Ruh-rarr?*" barked Oswald.

Sheila nodded. "While you look for the children. We're going to ask around and see if we can find out about this 'Izzy' person you were going on about."

Nina thanked Sheila, who quickly went to retrieve some of the missing children's clothes. Han and Greta's daddy brought over a pair of shorts belonging to his son and a cardigan that was his daughter's favourite. Oswald shoved his wolf-nose into each of them in turn and gave them a long, snuffling, sniff.

Once he was sure he had memorised the scent of the two children, Oswald put his snout into the breeze that was lightly wafting the leaves and took a deep, deep breath. Nina and Ivy looked on nervously, waiting, hoping that Oswald would catch the scent. They needn't have worried. Oswald caught a whiff of something interesting and, in a flash, he bounded off into the woods.

8

Where Wolf?

Oswald had to admit that he was enjoying some parts of being all werewolfed-up. In P.E. at school he always struggled to keep up with the other children. He wanted to do well, of course, the same as he did with all of his other classes, but no matter how hard he tried he never seemed to get any faster, or to score any more goals, or points. In fact, the whole idea of P.E. seemed like a complete and utter waste of time to him. Time that could be much better used learning something useful. From a book.

Being a werewolf had given him a whole different perspective on P.E. Now he could run at such a speed it felt like he was running as fast as a car. As his four paws thundered across the forest floor the trees were tearing past in a complete blur, but somehow the werewolf part of his brain was making sure he didn't run into a tree or trip over a root or a rock. Oswald galloped forward, his nose catching scents he never believed possible, the plants, the other animals... even Han and Greta.

He decided to see precisely how fast he could run. Faster and faster he galloped, his paws pounding quicker and quicker as he ploughed forward through the trees until first his trousers, then his t-shirt caught on branches and tore off his body...

He skidded to a stop, panting, his long, pink tongue hanging from between pointed teeth. He looked back at his human clothes and gave himself a shake, the same way he'd seen dogs shake when they came out of the sea. His fur felt even better uncovered and he pushed his nose into the air, sniffing for the scent of the children. It had grown more faint. He had run too far. Oswald knew that he had to be careful but he also knew now, more than ever, that P.E. really was a complete and utter waste of time. Once he got back to being a boy again he would never be able to run as fast as a car. And if he wasn't running as fast as a car, what was the point?

Catching the scent of the children once more, Oswald gave a little *woof* then set off, not quite as fast as a car, in the direction his nose told him the children had gone. It was odd, he thought as he hurtled headlong through the undergrowth, that the more the wolf blood pumped through his veins, the more hungry he was becoming and the more he had to keep reminding himself that he was a boy who had turned into a wolf and not a wolf who'd dreamed he was a boy.

The boy Oswald came crashing back in control when the wolf skidded to a halt. He was back where he, Ivy and Nina had all first appeared, in the clearing next to the witch's gingerbread house. His nose was telling him that Han and Greta were somewhere close by and, if they were, he had to find them before they encountered the witch and something terrible happened to them too.

"I'm sure no-one would mind if we broke off a tiny piece of the window," said a boy's voice. "Just for a little taste."

"I'm so hungry," said a girl's voice. "I'm certain it would be fine."

Oswald gave a mournful howl and the two voices fell silent. He sniffed the air before trotting around to the side of the house, where he saw two children.

That's them! He thought. *Now all I need to do is turn back into myself, explain and I can take them home.*

Oswald trotted forward and concentrated hard but, try as he might, he couldn't become a boy again. He stepped closer to the boy and the girl, who were dressed in the same old-fashioned clothes that the villagers had been wearing, and dipped his nose towards the ground, trying to show them he meant them no harm. The problem was that he wasn't a cute little dog, he was an enormous, hairy, wolf and it was difficult to be cute and cuddly when you looked like you might very well chomp someone's arm off and wander off with it into the woods.

"I think he's friendly," said the girl, reaching towards Oswald.

"No, Greta!" the boy grabbed her hand, pulling it away. "He might bite!"

Oswald tried once again to turn back into a boy but with every passing moment it became harder and harder. For now, at least, he was stuck as a wolf, so he did the only thing he could think of doing that would make the children trust him.

He ran off into the trees, grabbed a stick

in his mouth and scampered back to the brother and sister, dropping it at their feet. The children looked at the stick as if it might explode, so Oswald gave it a little nudge with his nose and then took a couple of steps away from them.

"You… you want me to throw it?" asked Greta.

Oswald gave the friendliest bark he could muster.

Han tentatively grabbed the stick and waved it in the air above Oswald's nose. Oswald wagged his tail and waited then, suddenly, Han threw the stick. Oswald's wolf-instincts took over and he bounded to the stick, bringing it back and dropping it at the siblings' feet once more.

After a few minutes playing fetch, Oswald

knew that he had to get the children to go with him, so he rolled over onto his back, throwing his paws in the air. Greta dove straight in, rubbing his tummy, and was quickly followed by Han, who tickled Oswald under his chin. Oswald rolled over and over, wagging his tail harder and harder, and with each wag the thought that he had to take the children back to their parents seemed to float further and further away.

He had to do something, and do it quickly. And then he remembered the white stones that he, Ivy and Nina had followed. Hopping back on to all four paws, Oswald galloped into the woods and came back with a white stone, about the size of a gobstopper, and dropped it at Han and Greta's feet.

"What's that, boy?" asked Greta with a smile. "What have you found?"

Oswald bounded off and grabbed another, dropping it a little closer to the woods, then another, then another. Soon there was a trail of the white stones that led all the way from the witch's house to the point where the path to the village widened out.

"He's trying to get us to follow him," said Greta, grabbing her brother's hand. "Come on!"

9

If The Wind Changes You'll Stay Like That

Back at the village, Nina and Ivy had been trying their best to pretend they were normal girls instead of a ghost and a vampire. But it wasn't entirely working. Sheila and a group of other adults who had gathered in front of the bookshop seemed to be quite happy to talk to them but other people kept their distance. Some walked past, muttering under their breath to one another, and a few annoying children kept running up behind Ivy and throwing pebbles through her.

"I think it's very rude to throw stones through a person," said Ivy, getting quite snippy.

Nina nodded and tried not to laugh, but was thankfully interrupted by one of the villagers coming over to tell them some news.

"The blacksmith says that Van Helsing was in yesterday after his horse threw a shoe," said the man. He was talking to Sheila and the others but his eyes kept flashing across to Nina and Ivy in a worried way. "He says that the horse was pulling a cart and the cart had a cover over it."

"And how does that help us, exactly?" asked Sheila.

"Well," the man continued. "Van Helsing was talking to someone or *some thing* under the cover and the blacksmith says that he called whoever it was 'Izzy'."

Nina was about to question the man further when one of the crowd gave a shout.

"Look, it's the wolf! And on his back..."

Nina and Ivy turned to see Oswald the werewolf trotting out of the forest at the exact spot they had arrived in the village, and on his back were two children. A boy and a girl.

"Han," a man's voice shouted. "Greta! You found them!"

"Thank goodness for that," Ivy whispered to Nina. "I was getting a little worried."

Nina nodded and ran over to greet Oswald and the children.

I won't spend too long telling you what happened next with Han and Greta. Not that it isn't an interesting story, don't get me wrong. It's just that it's not our story. Our story is about Nina, Ivy and Oswald and right now the sun is plummeting toward the horizon and the moon is rising in the sky and they don't have much time before the witch's spell becomes permanent but...

What's that?

Oh, very well... Han and Greta... But only for a moment... Because soon you'll want to know about Oswald being stuck in wolf-form too, won't you?

Once Han and Greta were sure they could trust the wolf (who we know was Oswald) they followed him but, because they had not eaten for so long, they were weak. Of course, as a wolf, Oswald could easily carry the children on his back like a big, shaggy, pony, so they hopped up and he carefully padded his way back along the white stone path to the village.

As they arrived back, Han and Greta's daddy raced to greet them and swept them up into his arms with kisses and cuddles. Their mother, however, was nowhere to be seen. As it happened, Han and Greta were soon telling their father a very worrying story indeed. The children had not wandered off themselves. In fact, their mother had led them deep into the woods on the first day. She had told them to wait in a clearing while she gathered firewood, and then she had left the children to be eaten by wild animals.

When Han and Greta's daddy confronted their mother she cried and cried, but the villagers all knew that she was a greedy woman and that the tears were not real tears but the tears of someone who loved money more than her own babies. In the days before Han and Greta's disappearance, their father had inherited a modest sum of money and, preferring to spend the cash on dresses and jewels rather than clothes and toys, she had hatched a plan to rid herself of the children once and for all.

When the truth came to light Han and Greta's daddy didn't hesitate in calling the authorities and their mother was thrown in prison for the rest of her days, as was customary in stories of this kind. Frankly she was lucky it wasn't a different sort of story, because she could have come out of the whole thing a lot worse.

Now can we please get back to poor old

Oswald?

Thank you.

Once Han and Greta had clambered off Oswald's back he trotted over to Ivy and Nina and gave them a half-hearted *woof*.

"What's the matter, Oswald?" asked Ivy.

Oswald whined, his head hanging forward.

"Why don't you change back to being a boy?" Nina chimed in.

Ivy looked him up and down and said, "I don't think he can. Can you turn back, Oswald?"

Oswald shook his head and then, glimpsing the bookshop behind them, he once more burst into life, running away from the girls and through the door of the bookshop.

10

Ghost-Girl, Wolf-Boy and Bat-Girl

"Even when he's a dog he still wants to hang around bookshops like a bad smell," said Nina.

Ivy smirked and the two girls stared at the shop, trying to make out what was going on inside through the tiny, filthy windows. After a minute or two there was a sound that might have been a table getting knocked over and then Oswald came trotting out of the shop, a book hanging from between his jaws.

"What've you got there?" Ivy asked.

Oswald wafted the open book towards her but Ivy just shrugged. "Can't grab it, dogface," she said. "I'm a ghost, remember?"

Oswald paused before turning to Nina and waggling the open book toward her. She took it from him and looked at the page he had been holding in his mouth.

"The full moon," she read from the book.

Oswald barked and sat on his hind legs, pointing one of his front paws at the sky. The girls looked up to the darkening blue sky and the full moon was already there, waiting for night to fall.

Nina skimmed down the page with her index finger.

"Tides… superstitions… ah, here we

are… werewolves."

Oswald gave a little *woof* of agreement.

"During a full moon a werewolf is unable to change into human form," Nina announced. "Oh dear, not so good for you then Oswald?"

Oswald shook his wolf head, then prodded at the book with his nose.

Nina kept reading until she came to the next part he was interested in. "Vampires… Oh, that's me! Vampires can't go out in the sunlight or they'll burst into flames."

The girls pondered this for a second, glancing up at the sun shining in the sky.

Oswald shook his head and prodded the book with his nose once more.

"Oh… right, there's more… unless it's a full moon, in which case they can walk day and night in complete safety," Nina concluded. "So good for me, not so good for you, Oswald?"

"But good news you can do that turning-into-a-bat thing and not worry about being batman after that?" said Ivy.

"Batman?" asked Nina.

"Bat-girl?" Ivy wondered.

"Bat-vamp-girl?" Nina added.

"Wuh-woof," Oswald barked.

"He's right, we should be on our way," said Ivy. "Time is ticking on."

"Is there anything else we can do for you lovely, lovely, children?" Sheila walked over, an enormous smile plastered across her face. "We really, truly, can never thank you enough. Here…" Sheila handed Nina a dog's lead. "In case you need it for your friend."

"Oh, erm, thank you," said Nina.

She took a map from her pocket, the map that Sheila had given her while Oswald had been off finding Han and Greta. It was frayed around the edges and yellowed with age but showed quite clearly the surrounding area. In the centre was the village itself, situated in a sheltered spot in a valley and surrounded by woods on all sides.

The children had come into the village from the south and, according to Sheila, if they followed the valley west they would eventually come across the castle of Van Helsing.

"So you're sure this Van Helsing character has Izzy?" asked Ivy, a little nervously. This was their only chance, and she didn't want to risk heading in the wrong direction. Just as the moon had affected Oswald, it also seemed to have an effect on her. The higher the moon rose, the more solid Ivy felt, as if she might even be able to move objects about once more, but as clouds passed over the moon she felt like she faded away. It was as if, when the moon was no longer shining, she wasn't a person or a ghost, she was a shadow.

"You can trust Sam," said Sheila with a reassuring smile. "He's not a gossip, not one to spread rumours, all he's doing is repaying your kindness. After what you children have done for us… We really are in your debt."

"I hope he's right," said Ivy, as she almost faded from view.

"Tell you what," said Nina. "Since you're

looking a little… pale, Ivy. And you're looking a little… erm, ruff, Oswald…"

"*Ruff*," barked Oswald.

Nina giggled. "Anyway, I really do have an idea. I'm going to turn into a bat, I'll fly west and check where we need to go. Once I'm sure we're heading in the right direction I'll fly back and tell you what I see. Sound like a plan?"

Oswald gave a loud *woof* then scratched behind his ear with his back leg.

Ivy said something, but her voice faded away into nothing.

"What was that?" said Nina, leaning in close to the faded ghost-shadow of her best friend.

"I said 'good idea'," Ivy's voice was as soft as a breeze blowing on a bag of feathers.

"I know it is," said Nina, giving her friends a wink.

She concentrated for a moment, then the vampire fangs extended in her mouth and finally, with a sound like a piece of paper being crumpled up, she rose into the air while shrinking and transforming into a small, black, bat.

Not wanting to waste any time, Nina fluttered away from her two friends and away from the village. She rose high into the air, still not quite sure of exactly how to work her bat-wings but fluttering them, beating them, to get higher and higher into the sky.

As she fluttered upwards she caught sight of the witch's house in the clearing to the south. She stared at it for a second but something caught her eye, something else in the sky. A large, white something that was travelling very fast. She hovered where she was, trying to work out what the creature was; her bat senses were giving her a lot of information, but it was different to people senses and she wasn't quite sure what to make of the creature beating its wings as it powered faster and faster towards her.

The clouds that had been covering the rising moon finally cleared and Ivy seemed to return to full visibility down on the ground.

"Oswald," she said. "Look at that…" Ivy pointed to the large, white, flapping creature tearing across the sky. "Is that… an owl?"

Oswald gave a short, sharp *woof* of

agreement.

"But don't owls eat bats?" Ivy went on.

Oswald gave a pitiful whine.

"Oh dear," said Ivy, as the owl swooped above their heads, grabbing bat-Nina in its talons before spiralling back higher into the air. "Oh no! Quick, Oswald," Ivy screamed. "Follow that owl!"

11

Follow That Owl

The animal kingdom is a dangerous world, my dear reader. You lead a lucky life. When you walk down the street with your mum or your dad there's almost no chance of you being scooped up by an enormous animal predator and eaten for their dinner.

It's a different story for most of the animals out there, though. Even the ones in your garden. Almost every animal you've ever seen has to be careful to avoid another, bigger animal that might eat it. For a bat, one of those animals is an owl, as Nina had found out to her peril.

Nina got an enormous shock when the owl swooped out of the sky and grabbed her in its sharp talons. Until that point she had fixed her gaze in the direction the castle of Van Helsing was supposed to be in. Unfortunately, she hadn't been able to spot it; in fact, in the spot the castle should have been stood a ramshackle-looking house. And then, suddenly…

Whoooooooosh

She was travelling in the same direction but at breakneck speed. Nina had no idea how a bat would act if they were grabbed by an owl, but she knew exactly how a vampire-girl would act. She turned back into a girl, right there in mid-air.

I would be very surprised indeed if you

had ever seen an owl flying through the air with a young girl in its talons, and there is a very simple reason for that: young girls are far too heavy for owls to carry. If an owl somehow managed to flap its wings hard enough to lift a child high in the air then, as soon as gravity realised what was going on both the girl and the owl would drop to the ground as fast as two large stones.

So, when Nina abruptly turned back into a girl what do you think happened?

You're absolutely correct. Nina plummeted downwards and the owl, whose talons were now caught in her trouser leg, plummeted just as quickly. As she dropped toward the ground a thought popped into Nina's head. *I'm not sure that was such a good idea,* was what she thought.

Luckily for her they were flying directly over the deep, dense, forest, so instead of hitting the hard ground, Nina and the owl hit a treetop.

And then they bounced onto another, slightly lower treetop.

Finally, they hit branch after leafy branch, bough after green bough, each one making them fall a little slower so that when Nina's bottom hit the ground she was travelling slowly enough to suffer nothing worse than a sore bum.

Of course, the whole of this very worrying incident was witnessed by Ivy and Oswald and neither of them wasted a second, moving as quickly as their legs would carry them to help their friend. Oswald bounded out once more, ducking and dodging left and right to avoid the deep, dense forest all around. Ivy quickly realised that trying to avoid the trees slowed her down so instead she ran in a completely straight line, finally embracing her ghostly abilities to simply pass through the trees.

In spite of the lack of light as they got deeper into the woods, it wasn't too difficult for Oswald and Ivy to locate their friend. They followed her voice. Falling out of the sky had made Nina very cross indeed and as they got closer to her they realised that she was telling someone off.

"Do you have any idea how very, very dangerous that was?" Nina's voice echoed through the woods.

As they drew closer, the sound grew louder, but Oswald found his path blocked by thick, thorny bushes. He skidded to a halt, turning to bark at Ivy who nodded and walked right through them.

"Nina!" Ivy shouted. "Are you okay?"

"Ivy!" said Nina. "No, I'm not okay. My bum is *really* sore. And it's this owl's fault." Nina pointed at a big, fluffy, pile of brown and white feathers.

The pile ruffled itself and opened two big, dark eyes.

"Hoo-who are you?" the pile of feathers twooted.

"Who, me?" asked Nina.

"Noo, you."

"Ooh, you," said Ivy. "You're an ool."

"An ool?"

"I mean an owl!" Ivy giggled. "I'm Ivy, I'm a ghost. At least for now."

Oswald bounded to Nina's side and gave a little *woof*.

"Are you okay?" Ivy asked.

The owl shook its feathers and drew itself up onto its legs. It turned its head left and right then extended its wings and gave them a flap.

"Ow-woo!" said the owl, folding its left wing back down. "No-woo, I've hurt my wing."

"Well, what do you expect if you go grabbing innocent girls mid-air?," Nina stamped her foot.

"How-woo was I to know who you were?" asked the owl.

"The owl's got a point," said Ivy, nodding in agreement.

Nina grumbled under her breath and

rubbed her arm, which was also sore.

"Woof!" said Oswald.

"Oh yes, good point," agreed Ivy, somehow understanding what Oswald was saying. "Did you see Van Helsing's castle?"

Nina shook her head. "Afraid not," said Nina. "There's a house over there but no castle."

"Twit-twoo," said the owl, giving its wings another flap. "That house *is* Van Helsing's. And I think my wing is fine thank you-hoo."

"Oh right," said Nina. "Well, I'm glad you're not badly hurt, Mr Owl."

"Mrs."

"Sorry – Mrs Owl."

The owl flapped her wings and took off once more. "Good luck to you-hoo!" she cooed before flying out of sight.

"Come on then," said Nina. "It's not far. Maybe we can get ourselves turned back after all!"

12

The Castle Of Van Helsing

As Mrs Owl circled overhead, stretching her wings once more (and probably looking for some bats who weren't girls to eat), the children made their way west through the dense woods. The trees were so close together that it was difficult for Nina and Oswald to find a path. Ivy didn't have a problem, of course, as she slipped right through the trees, leading the way and encouraging the others to hurry along.

The sun was getting lower and lower in the sky and the full moon was clearly visible, rising higher and higher with each passing minute. The clouds that had been so bothersome to Ivy earlier had also given up trying to hide their friend the moon and the sky was now completely and utterly clear.

"How long do you think we've got before midnight?" Nina asked Oswald as she tramped forward. Twigs snapped underfoot with every step but the forest seemed to be thinning a little as they went on.

"Ruh-roh?" barked Oswald.

"I wish I'd put a watch on," Nina continued. "But I suppose even that might not have been any use because what if it was a different time in the story to what time it was in the bookshop. Remember that time when we…"

"Oswald! Nina!" Ivy shouted from up

ahead. "It's here. We found it!"

Nina and Oswald rushed forward, pushing through branches that twanged back and thwacked them when they let go until they came upon the castle of Van Helsing.

"Well, that is the most rubbish castle I've ever seen," said Nina.

"Ruh-huh," agreed Oswald.

"I mean it looked pretty bad from the air but down here it's just... rubbish."

The 'castle' was a small, two storey house that probably had two or three downstairs rooms and a couple of bedrooms above. In fact, the only things that were castle-ish about it were that it had iron bars over the windows and a square tower attached at one side. Well, I say 'tower'... it was only slightly taller than the roof of the house itself and looked like it might be made from medieval Lego bricks.

"You should knock," said Ivy.

Nina approached the heavy wooden door and gave three loud bangs. "Mr Van Helsing?" she said in a loud, clear voice. "Are you in?"

There was a scampering noise from inside the house, the sound of someone quickly moving around. A moment later a panel in the door, which was also protected by iron bars, opened and a man's face peered out. The man's eyes were blue and he had reddish hair, that was brushed back out of his face, and a large, square chin.

"Halloo? Who are you?" He had a singsong voice that went up and down in pitch with every syllable. "What do you want with me?"

"Hello," said Ivy. "We are—"

The man screamed and slammed the hatch in the door shut.

Nina turned to Ivy. "I bet he could see through you. He probably got scared. Hang on…" She approached the door once more and gave another three loud bangs. "Mr Van Helsing?" she repeated. "We didn't mean to frighten you. Can we talk to you please?'

The panel in the door opened once more and the man peered out. This time he looked carefully at Ivy, then Nina, then Oswald in turn.

"No. Go away," he said and slammed the panel shut once more.

Oswald gave a little whine and his tail,

which had been proud and wagging behind him, was dipped down forlornly between his back legs.

"Urgh," said Ivy. "How come we always end up with someone who's doolally?"

Nina approached the door for a third time and gave three loud bangs. "Mr Van Helsing?" she said. "We know you're in there. We need your help. Please?"

There was no sound. No scampering about, no locking of doors. Nothing.

"What are we going to do?" asked Nina. "I honestly don't think he's going to open the door."

Ivy grinned a wicked grin.

"Doors?" she smiled. "Who needs doors?"

Nina suddenly realised what her friend

was thinking and a smile crept across her face too. "Oh yeah," she said.

Oswald gave an excited bark and jumped left and right, wagging his tail.

"What are you doing out there?" The singsongy voice sounded muffled but could still be heard from inside the little house. "Go away or I'll... erm... well... I'll... Oh I'm not sure. Just go away. Or I'll call... I'll call someone for help. I don't know who but I'll call someone!"

"Is it me or does he sound a bit Swedish to you?" asked Ivy with a giggle.

"What are you waiting for?" Nina reached to give her friend a shove but, remembering that she couldn't touch her, just wafted her hand in a kind of half-wave in front of her instead.

Ivy grinned even wider and took a couple of steps back before breaking into a sprint, running straight toward Van Helsing's front door.

"I'm warning you I'll call for help! I'll call for someone!"

Unfortunately, Ivy hadn't exactly been expecting to find Van Helsing himself huddled on the other side of the door, cowering with his back to her. Ivy ran straight through the door then straight through Van Helsing too, before skidding to a halt half way in and half way out of a table once more.

Van Helsing slowly drew himself up to his full height. He stared, wide-eyed at Ivy and raised both of his hands into the air, holding them up in front of his face. As he stared, a gooey jelly-like substance ran down and dripped from his hands. In fact, it wasn't only his hands. His hair was plastered to his head with goo, his face covered in gloop. From the tip of his nose to the tip of his toes he was covered with gunk, the ectoplasm from ghostly Ivy oozing and dripping off his whole, entire body.

"She slimed me!" he screamed.

"Meh," said Ivy giving a little shrug. "Who you gonna call?"

13

Van The Scaredy Cat Man

Van Helsing screamed. Ivy stared at him and smiled. Van Helsing kept screaming. Ivy kept staring and smiling. Van Helsing stopped screaming to take a breath.

"Are you going to do that all day or will you shut up for a while so I can talk to you?" asked Ivy.

Van Helsing gave Ivy a sheepish look as he dripped ectoplasm-goo on the floor. A ginger tomcat wandered over to Ivy and tried to sniff her. When he couldn't smell anything he gave Ivy a sideways look and wandered off.

"I should banish you, evil spirit!" Van Helsing squeaked.

Ivy shook her head. "I'm not an evil spirit."

"You're not?"

"I'm not."

"You're not going to drag me to the Hell dimensions and torment me for eternity?"

Ivy shook her head. "Pretty sure I'm not."

"Oh," said Van Helsing. "Okay. What do you want?"

And so Ivy tried her best to explain exactly what the children wanted. As Van Helsing cleaned the ghostly goo off himself, Ivy told him how they had been walking past the witch's house and she had accidentally turned them into monsters. She told him how they had gone to the village and helped out the villagers. She told him how Oswald was stuck as a werewolf. She told him that Nina was a vampire and even told him that she had been grabbed by an owl. She was about to tell him all about Izzy when he interrupted her.

"I will help you I think," he said in his up and down sing-song way. "Your friends. Tell them to come in. The vampire-girl, I invite her."

Ivy nodded and walked to the door to open it but remembered that she couldn't. "Erm… a little help?" she said.

"Ah, so sorry," Van Helsing said, striding over and flinging open the door. "Your friend has explained things. Come inside."

Oswald dived forward, bounding up to

Van Helsing and jumping up, putting his paws on the man's chest and licking his face.

"Yes, yes," Van Helsing said, pushing Oswald to the ground. "The full moon?"

Ivy nodded. "He's stuck like that."

"Pleased to meet you Mr Van Helsing," said Nina.

"Call me Van," said Van Helsing. "You have been day walking?"

Nina nodded.

"It is the full moon. Usually you would burst into flames in the day," said Van Helsing then, suddenly taking a step away from Nina, he continued. "Were you looking at my neck? She was looking at my neck. That vampire-girl wants to bite me!"

Van Helsing screamed.

"No she doesn't," said Ivy. "Do you

Nina?"

Nina licked her lips and said nothing.

Oswald kept wagging his tail and staring at Van Helsing.

"It's fine, Van," said Ivy. "So, everyone, Van thinks he can help us."

Nina smiled and licked her teeth menacingly at him.

"Erm," said Van Helsing. "Please, follow me."

The children followed him to a door in the corner of the room which led to a flight of rickety stairs. While Van Helsing strode off in front, they followed, being careful not to trip. At the top of the stairs was a corridor with one door on either side and one at the end.

"That is my room," he said, pointing to

the left. "I will show you your room but you must never, ever, ever go in the room at the end of the corridor. Do you understand?"

"Hang on a second," said Nina, suddenly realising what Van Helsing was saying. "What do you mean 'our room'?"

"If I am going to be helping you...you will be here for a while."

"How long's a while?" asked Nina.

Van Helsing shrugged. "The last time I did a spell like this it didn't take long."

"See," said Ivy. "Nothing to worry about."

"Probably only a year or two."

"What?" chorused Nina and Ivy.

"*Ruh?*" barked Oswald.

"Yes, yes, not much more than a couple of years," Van Helsing confirmed.

Suddenly there was a scratching at the door at the end of the corridor, the door that Van Helsing had told the children never to open. Much to Nina and Ivy's surprise, Oswald bolted down the hallway, skidding to a halt in front of the door and growling and barking madly at it.

"Oswald!" shouted Nina. "Stop that!"

Oswald stopped being quite as frantic but was still barking loudly at the door.

"Oswald!" Nina shouted even louder. "Shut up or I'll throw you down a well!"

Oswald made a whining noise but stayed stock still, staring at the door.

"This is all getting a bit out of hand," Nina stamped her foot on the wooden floor and pointed her index finger at Van Helsing. "We appreciate your offer to help but... two years? We can't hang around here for two years! The witch said that she could cure us today…"

"The witch?!" Van Helsing squeaked. "She must be stopped, she—"

"Never mind all that," said Nina.

"But—"

Nina vamped out, making her front teeth all pointy and glaring at Van Helsing.

"Sorry," he said in a very quiet voice indeed.

"The witch said she could turn us back if we brought Izzy back to her," said Nina.

"And people in the village said you've got Izzy," added Ivy.

Oswald gave another bark at the door.

"Oswald's right," said Nina. "Seems highly likely Izzy is locked in the tower."

Van Helsing whimpered.

"Speak up!" snapped Nina.

"She is," Van Helsing nodded. "I took Izzy from the witch to use in my experiments. And so she couldn't use her in her evil spells."

"You've got it all wrong," said Ivy in a more kindly tone. "The witch isn't evil. She's just a bit useless."

Van Helsing stared at Ivy, thinking about what the children had said. As he stood there the scratching started again, louder this time. Oswald stared at the door, poised, ready to pounce, to take down whoever it was on the other side. Nina reached forward to the door knob and Van Helsing gave a half-hearted nod.

Nina looked to Ivy, who gave her a

friendly smile and a nod. She gripped the door knob tightly and slowly turned it.

14

You're Coming With Us

The door was heavy and as it creaked open the dank, musty smells of the tower escaped and filled the children's noses. They stared into the darkness and a moment later a purring noise could be heard before a small, black, cat scampered forward and rubbed itself against Nina's legs.

"Awww!" said Nina, reaching down to stroke the cat. "Are you Izzy's cat?"

"What are you talking about?" asked Van Helsing. "That is Izzy."

"That's Izzy?" asked Ivy. "You stole a

131

witch's cat?"

"Stole is a very strong word," said Van Helsing. "I took the cat from the witch to stop her doing magic. And so I could use her in my research."

"But what I don't understand is why you wanted her to stop doing magic," said Ivy. "She was only cross because her magic was going wrong and it was only going wrong because you took her cat!"

Van Helsing grumbled under his breath. Oswald barked at him and Izzy scampered behind Nina's legs to hide.

"She put a spell on my roses," said Van Helsing, an angry frown draped across his brow.

"What?" Nina and Ivy chorused.

"Why would she do that?" asked Ivy.

"Well, I don't know, do I?" Van Helsing blurted. "I woke up one morning and my roses were covered in bugs."

"Little green bugs?" asked Nina as she picked up Izzy and gave her a tickle under the chin.

"How did you know?" asked Van Helsing.

"They're called aphids," said Nina. "My mum has them on her roses sometimes. They're just bugs that like roses... not magic. Just bugs."

"Well... erm..." Van Helsing's face went bright red.

"I think you need to apologise to that poor woman," said Nina.

Ivy nodded in agreement. "And we're going to have to get a move on, look..." She pointed out of the window; the sun had set.

"Yes," said Nina. "We don't have long. We need to get to the witch quickly or we really will be staying with you for the next few years."

Nina, Ivy and Oswald made their way back downstairs with Nina carrying Izzy inside her coat and Van Helsing trailing grumpily behind them.

"Aren't you going to put some shoes on?" asked Ivy as the children left the house.

Van Helsing looked down at his slippers then looked at the deep forest that surrounded them,

"No," he said, leaving the house and locking the door behind them.

The full moon shone down on the ghost, the vampire and the werewolf, lighting their way like an electric floodlight. If you had been a grumpy owl, flying hungrily over the forest, you would have seen the three friends quickly picking their way through, heading back to the village, followed closely by the grumbling Van Helsing. Except that the owl had given up for the night and would try again tomorrow, when she hoped that there would be a smaller chance of accidentally picking up a vampire-girl instead of a bat.

The gang picked their way through the trees and undergrowth and soon they arrived back in front of the bookshop near the blacksmith's in the village.

"Hello?" called Nina.

"Anyone here?" Van Helsing's singsong voice shouted.

The words echoed around the village

square but there was no reply.

"Perhaps they are in the tavern?" said Van Helsing, pointing over to a large building with a sign hanging outside. "We should go in and drink some ale. And if there's no-one there we won't have to pay."

Nina and Ivy scowled as Van Helsing waltzed towards the tavern.

"Oi!" shouted Ivy. "You're not going in there!"

"But-but…" Van Helsing pointed to the sign.

"The Laughter Lamb?" Nina wondered aloud. "What does that even mean?"

"Some of the letters have worn off, I think," said Ivy. "I think it's supposed to say 'slaughtered'."

"What? Are you threatening me now?"

said Van Helsing, running in a panic back towards the children. "I am not going to become a victim of your carnivorous lunar activities!"

"What is he on about?" asked Ivy as Van Helsing ran away from the tavern.

"Ooh... I've got an idea," said Nina. "Oswald, is there a scent you can pick up on? To track where everyone's gone?"

Oswald sniffed the air. He turned his head a little to the left, lifted his nose a touch higher and sniffed again, then he let out a wolf-woof that was so loud Nina could feel it echoing in her chest.

"He has the wolf senses?" asked Van Helsing.

Ivy nodded, her eyes fixed on Oswald. Bathed in the glow of the moonlight he looked quite scary.

And then he let out the howl… the full-throated wolf *Awooooooooooooooooooooh*.

His jaws snapped closed with a noise like two wooden planks snapping together. The girls said nothing, just stared into the woods in the direction Oswald was trotting.

"We're off to see the witch then…" Ivy muttered under her breath.

"The wonderful witch of odd…" added Nina, forgetting to smile as she stared into the pitch black of the woods. "I'm a bit scared." She reached inside her coat to the pouch she had tucked Izzy in and gave the little cat a stroke.

"Pah!" Van Helsing shuffled off after Oswald. "What have *you* got to be scared of? You're a vampire, silly girl!"

"Oh yeah!" said Nina with a grin. "Come on then!"

She and Ivy ran after Oswald and Van Helsing, the four of them soon coming across the white pebbled path and following it quickly through the woods. The closer they came to the witch's house, the more noise could be heard; people nervously whispering in the distance, branches breaking under foot. The villagers were on their way to see the witch and Nina and Ivy had a bad feeling about what the results would be.

When they were close enough to see the flames from the villagers' torches Nina curled her index finger and thumb together, put them between her lips and gave a short, sharp, whistle. Oswald trotted back to her side and Ivy and Van Helsing gathered too.

"Does anyone know what time it is?" she asked.

Van Helsing took a fob watch out of his waistcoat pocket and took a look at it. "A quarter to eleven."

Ivy yawned.

"Don't start that, you'll set us all off," Nina scolded. "We haven't got long before we're stuck like this so we need to hurry, but I think we should go around the side of the house."

Oswald yawned a big, open-mouthed doggie yawn that showed not just his big, pink tongue but also his enormous wolf-fangs.

"You've set him off now…" said Nina, rolling her eyes.

"Go around the side?" said Ivy, trying to change the subject.

"Good idea," said Van Helsing. "You take wolfie. I'll take Ivy."

Nina gave Oswald a tickle behind the ear and he wagged his tail. "Okay, let's go!"

And off they went; Ivy and Van Helsing to the left and Nina, Izzy and Oswald to the right. Before they could get into position they heard shouting. It was the villagers. They had gathered the mob in front of the witch's house but instead of the terrible and useless things they had carried the last time they were a lot more prepared.

They carried flaming torches. They carried pointy sticks. And they carried pitchforks.

Nina groaned to herself. "I should never have told them they were a rubbish mob," she said to Oswald, who whined in agreement.

"Come out and be burned at the stake!" a man shouted at the witch.

"Don't be daft," the witch's voice came from inside the house. "Why would I come out if you're going to burn me at the stake?"

There was a muttering in the crowd with no-one really knowing how to reply.

"Good point," the man shouted again. "Well, stay where you are. We're going to burn your house down with you inside."

Izzy gave a pitiful *meow* from inside Nina's coat but Nina was too busy whispering in Oswald's ear to notice.

"Right then!" the witch shouted back. "Give it your best try you great berk!"

"Berk?" the man muttered. "I'll show

you." In his hand he held a heavy branch with a rag dipped in oil wrapped around one end. He reached forward with the stick and touched one of the other villager's torches; the rag instantly burst into flames. Once he was happy that it was burning well he pulled it back and then hurled it into the air, straight at the witch's house.

15

Time Is Running Out

The burning torch cartwheeled towards the gingerbread house but Oswald was already bounding toward it. He moved like lightning, pouncing high into the air and, with a crunch, caught the stick in his mouth before it had a chance to hit the witch's gingerbread house.

He dropped the flaming stick in the grass and dragged it this way and that, putting out the flame completely.

"Haha!" came the witch's voice from inside the house.

Nina, Ivy and Van Helsing all ran forward to Oswald's side, Nina cradling Izzy in her arms. The black cat didn't like being held and, realising it was home, struggled and jumped down to the ground before darting around to the side of the house.

"Is that you three again?" came a friendlier, female voice from the crowd.

"Sheila?" Ivy asked and, sure enough, out of the crowd stepped the kindly woman who had helped them earlier in the day. Except now she was carrying an enormous pointy stick that looked very much like it had once been a rolling pin.

"Hi kids," Sheila said with a smile. "You come to help?"

"Help?" asked Nina.

"It's Halloween, remember?" said Sheila.

"Yes?"

"Well, we thought we'd take your advice and..."

"Nononono..." Nina interrupted. "You've got it all wrong..."

"But you said that we needed better weapons and the witch..."

"No!" Nina snapped. "You can't go around burning people to death. You just can't. And anyway, this isn't a bad witch, I think she's misunderstood."

Sheila lowered her knife to her side. "Is this right, Van Helsing?"

"Maybe," he replied. Oswald gave him a shove with his nose. "Yes. Misunderstood."

"And besides that," said Ivy. "Don't you realise what happens when you set fire to sugar?"

The crowd grumbled that it didn't know.

"Well I know," said Ivy. "If you set fire to sugar it caramelises. And this is a house made of sweeties."

"Ah," said Sheila. "You're right."

Ivy nodded.

Suddenly, the door of the witch's house burst open and there, all green-skinned and brandishing her wand in front of her, was the witch. The mob of villagers gasped.

"That's what I'm talking about," said the witch. "Never mind me throwing a Halloween party, I think now that I've got my cat back I'm going to turn all of you lot into…"

"Erm, Belinda?" said Nina who had snuck up on the witch and was now pulling at her sleeve.

"What?" snapped the witch.

"Look at the time," said Nina.

"I haven't got a watch," replied the witch.

Izzy came trotting out of the house and began rubbing herself against Nina's legs and purring.

"Stop that, Izzy!" Belinda the witch bellowed.

The cat looked up at her and might have smiled, ignoring what the witch was saying as it continued to purr against Nina's legs.

"Does anyone have the right time?" Belinda sighed as she scanned her eyes left and right, trying to spot someone who had a watch. "No-one? Really?" She turned back to Nina. "Why do you want to know the time, deary?"

"Because we'll be stuck as monsters if you

don't turn us back before midnight," Ivy said, getting louder with every word until, by the end of the sentence, she was shouting at the witch.

"Oh yes," said Belinda. "Forgot about that in all this excitement. But I can't leave this lot out here, they might burn the place down."

Oswald gave a bark and bounded out toward the villagers.

"You know, I think I can almost understand him now, maybe we don't need to turn him back," said Nina with a giggle.

Oswald growled at her.

"Only kidding!" Nina grinned. "You said something about a party. How about you wave your wand and set up the party for *everyone* out here."

The witch looked at Nina. Then she looked at the crowd.

"Oh alright," the witch said eventually. "A party's no fun if you're on your own, but you have to promise he'll be here when we come back." Belinda leaned over to Van Helsing and prodded her finger playfully at his shoulder. "You big hunk of handsome."

Van Helsing's mouth moved up and down but no sounds came out.

"He'll be here," said Ivy sweetly, then turning to Van Helsing she growled, "won't you?!"

Van Helsing nodded and tried to smile back at the witch.

"Oh goody," said the witch. She waved her wand and the clearing that surrounded her house burst into life with magical streamers launching themselves from tree to tree. Lanterns appeared to grow from the boughs of the trees and spilled multi-coloured light everywhere. Chairs and tables appeared before tablecloths floated down from the darkness above and all kinds of food and drink popped into existence like popcorn bursting from invisible kernels.

The crowd gave an impressed "oooh" before a mist blew through the clearing and left behind the Halloween decorations. Spooky skulls and skeletons, a barrel of apples for bobbing and lots more besides. In the meantime the witch had been busily preparing the reversing spell in her scullery. But I can't really tell you all the details. You see, the spell the witch was casting was a bit dangerous and I don't want any of the grown-ups in your house finding out I taught you how to turn someone into a dog. They'd probably throw me into the sea if they found out.

And so the witch had prepared the ingredients in her cauldron and as the clock ticked towards midnight she began to chant…

"Spirits of the ground, spirits of the air,

Rid us of the ghost and the werewolf over there.

Take the vampire and make her go away,

Turn them back to normal while it's still today."

There was a rumble of thunder in the distance and the house shook.

"Spirits of the sea, spirits of the borange,

Now I come to think of it, turn me back

to orange."

There was a flash of light and a noise that sounded like *whurp ping!* The children turned to see what was going on and as they did a pink mist flew out of the cauldron and zapped straight into them.

Nina, Ivy, Oswald and Belinda the witch were knocked to the ground like pins in a bowling alley.

16

What Colour Are Witches?

"Ugh," said Oswald. "Are you alright?"

"Oswald?" chorused the girls.

There was a crashing of furniture as everyone blinked their eyes open once more.

"Is everyone okay?" asked Belinda, whose skin was now a quite lovely shade of orange.

"Oswald, are you okay?" asked Nina. "Can you speak? Are you a boy again?"

Belinda went and opened a nearby cupboard. She took out some clothes.

"He's fine, he's a boy again," said Belinda. "But he's a boy who's in the nuddy now."

"What?" asked Ivy, stepping backwards and crashing into a chair. "I can touch things again! I'm not a ghost anymore!"

"Well you see," continued Belinda. "All that running about in the woods... even the magic only stretches so far..."

"He's naked?" asked Ivy.

"Eew!" giggled the girls.

"Luckily I've collected one or two things over the years. I'm sure these will be about the right size. Here you go my lad."

Nina put his glasses on the table and the girls turned their backs. They could hear struggling as Oswald pulled on the remainder of his clothes.

"You can turn around now," he said once he was dressed.

The girls turned around to see their

Oswald. All in one piece and pushing his glasses up his nose once more.

"I have to ask," said Oswald. "What does 'borange' mean? When you were saying the rhyme you said 'borange'."

Belinda shrugged and waved her wand in the air. Sparks flew from it, landing in Izzy's black fur as she rubbed against her mistress's legs. "It has to rhyme. I had to get something to rhyme with orange. Nothing does."

"I have two questions," interrupted Nina.

"Yes?"

"One – 'orange' rhymes with 'orange'. Why not just say it twice?"

"Oh, I suppose I could have. Well, maybe next time."

"Two – why do you want to be orange?"

"Well, what colour do you expect me to be?" cackled Belinda. "Red?" She roared with laughter.

"So all witches are orange?" asked Oswald with genuine interest.

Belinda shook her head. "No, not all of them. But all women with orange skin are witches."

There was a rustling in the woods out the back of the house and Oswald spun around to see what was making the noise.

"Did you see what it was?" asked Ivy, a little nervously.

Oswald was frowning. "I think…" he paused, wracking his brain. "I might have seen your Uncle Bill, Nina."

"We have to go," said Nina in a panic. "Belinda. Thank you. Be nice to the villagers, enjoy the party and don't cast any nasty spells. Do you promise?"

Belinda nodded, then stared through the opposite window at the party that was unfolding out there. She gazed at Van Helsing and took her lipstick from a drawer.

"Oh I promise," she said, puckering her lips and painting them bright red with the lipstick. "I thought I saw romance in my tea leaves the last time I read them and now my heart is a flutter for that hunk out there."

"Riiiiiight," said Nina. "Not sure we need to know more than that. Don't want to have to wash our brains to get rid of any horrible memories now do we?"

Belinda wasn't listening. She was near the window blowing kisses at Van Helsing who, for some reason, seemed to be blowing kisses at the strange orange woman staring back at him.

Nina threw open the back door and the three children ran out towards the woods at the back of the house, but the moment they stepped out of the clearing and into the woods a cloud passed over the moon and they were plunged into pitch blackness. Out of nowhere leaves and soil from the forest floor began swirling around them, faster and faster it spun, getting thicker and thicker until, with a thunderous bang, everything stopped and everything went dark

17

Back To
The Lost Bookshop

When they opened their eyes the friends were back in the hidden room in the Lost Bookshop. Books were scattered all around them like leaves fallen from book trees.

"I forgot to check," said Ivy eventually. "Did the witch turn you back to normal or not, Nina."

Nina pretended to lunge over to bite Ivy's neck but gave her a hug instead. "I think I'm cured," she said.

"Look!" said Oswald. He held up a book.

A book called 'The Witch With the Glitch'. On the cover were a whole host of fantastical illustrations, but in the middle was a witch, half green, half orange, and next to her were three children. And each child cast a different shadow. One shadow was in the shape of a ghost, another a vampire and the third a werewolf.

Both Nina and Ivy reached out, touching the old cloth of the cover and flicking through the pages, before Oswald placed it carefully back on the shelf they had chosen. Their shelf in the hidden room.

"Nina? Ivy? Oswald?" a voice called from somewhere else in the bookshop. It was muffled, far away, but unmistakably Nina's Aunty Ann.

The children slipped out of the hidden

room, locking the door behind them and dashing into the corridor.

"You three been busy?" Nina's Uncle Bill appeared from somewhere. "Did you get all of those books sorted out I asked you to?"

The three friends nodded.

"Good," said Uncle Bill with a smile. "Now go and find your Aunty Ann, she told me she was making hot chocolates with marshmallows in. You don't want them to get cold, do you?"

"Noooo!" Ivy and Oswald raced off down the corridor.

"Thank you," Nina said, giving her Uncle Bill a big, beaming smile. "I love it here."

Uncle Bill nodded and smiled, took his glasses off and rubbed them on his sleeve.

The two of them said nothing for a

moment. Uncle Bill put his glasses back on and pointed at the floor.

"You dropped something," he said.

Nina looked down at the floor and there was a set of false plastic vampire teeth, the kind you slip over your own teeth to pretend to be a vampire.

"I've just thought of the best prank," Nina began, but when she looked up, Uncle Bill had gone.

Nina grabbed the teeth and, giggling, put them into her mouth before running off after her friends.

No-one else knew about the adventure they had in the hidden room in the Lost Bookshop. No-one in the world.

But the children knew. And I know. And you know.

And Aunty Ann and Uncle Bill?

Well, you never know what they know.

The End?

It may be the end of the book but the Lost Bookshop adventures are just beginning…

The next book in the series is 'The Mystery of the Missing Monkey' and you can find out all about it here:

www.adammaxwell.com/lost1

Thank You

Don't worry, you haven't stumbled into a hidden chapter of the Lost Bookshop, this is just the page where I take the opportunity to thank a few people who helped in the process of this book being sneezed onto the page.

As always, bringing a book to life takes a lot of hard work so I just wanted to say thank you to everyone who helped.

Dale Maloney whose covers just get better and better.

Sam Hartburn and Elaine Jinks-Turner for being phenomenal co-editors without even realising it.

Brenda West and Oliver Kinsley for beta-reading the living heck out of the book and telling me when I spelled things wrong and when I was using gibberish instead of sentences.

To my wonderful wife Eve whose encouragement and love is the fire under my creative butt. In a good way.

Lastly thank you to the real Aunty Ann and Uncle Bill - owners of the finest fictional bookshop in the world.

Printed in Poland
by Amazon Fulfillment
Poland Sp. z o.o., Wrocław